FRANKIE SPARROW
and the Crinklebottom Curse

Ewan McGregor

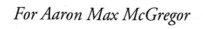

For Aaron Max McGregor

CHAPTER 1

Start with a bang!

Frankie Sparrow flew as fast as his wings would take him. The rain lashed down and this made the chase even trickier than usual. The suspect was doing exactly as Frankie and his Uncle Charlie had thought he would. Some magpies - the one's with no self-control, the ones who caused most of the crime and gave magpies their bad reputation - were easy to predict. Shiny things. That's what they went after and today was no different.

The magpie had stolen keys from Mrs Campbell's door. The same Mrs Campbell who kept the bird feeder in her garden well stocked for birds, including Uncle Charlie. The magpie had done it twice before, so the two private investigators had taken it upon themselves to set up a surveillance operation. It hadn't taken them long to get a result. This magpie wasn't exactly a master criminal.

Frankie followed the suspect at a safe distance so as he wouldn't be spotted. His feathers were soaked through. He had followed the magpie from the moment he'd watched him snatch Mrs Campbell's house key from her porch door.

Frankie ducked and weaved in and out of the trees. The magpie was fast, Frankie was faster. The magpie was large and exposed, Frankie was small and inconspicuous. There was no way Frankie was going to lose sight of him.

The two sparrows both knew where the magpie's nest was located, and they knew that was exactly where he was headed. Uncle Charlie lay in wait near the entrance to the nest, camouflaged by the trees and sheltered from the heavy rain.

Just as the large black and white bird was making the turn to the entrance of his nest Frankie flew into action. He increased his pace until he was right on the magpie's tail. He sped up further and came alongside the large bird before the magpie had even noticed there was anyone there.

'STOP!!!' Frankie shouted as loud as he could, right into the thief's ear. The magpie was shocked, he'd thought he was alone. Frankie had given him a huge fright and now Charlie, on Frankie's signal had appeared from the trees. He gathered up a head of steam and flew as fast as he could. He barged right into the much larger bird.

Shocked and now startled, the magpie started to spiral out of control. He was spinning round and round. The rain made it even harder to stop. He had completely lost control. Faster and faster he spun! He was going to crash! The magpie's pace increased; he had no chance to steady himself. He spun and spun until BANG!!! The magpie came to a bone crunching stop with a loud crash and a thud against his nest door.

There were black and white feathers everywhere. The stolen keys which were being carried by the now dazed and confused bird flew into the air. Frankie caught them in his beak.

The magpie's nest door had opened with the force of its owner crashing into it and two more sets of Mrs Campbell's keys spilled out. Frankie grasped one set in his wing. Uncle Charlie grabbed the other set with his beak. Perfect. Mrs Campbell would be pleased.

The magpie sat against his nest defeated - he was soaked with the rain and sore from the crash. Even worse, he had been defeated by two little sparrows. If his friends found out about this it would be beyond embarrassing.

Frankie and Charlie's plan had worked a treat.

They both congratulated each other on a job well done. Another case quickly solved by Charlie and Frankie Sparrow: Private Investigator's.

CHAPTER 2
The case is on

'Frankie Sparrow, could you stay behind after class?'
Mr Finch said.

Frankie's classmates laughed as they filed out of the
room. They were used to seeing Frankie getting into
trouble. The thing was though, Frankie *really* hadn't
done anything wrong this time, he was 100% certain
of it.

'Don't look so worried Frankie. I asked you to stay
behind to say well done. Your schoolwork is fairly
coming on. Keep up the good work!' Mr Finch said.

'Erm… thanks.' Frankie said. He couldn't believe
his ears. He had never received praise from any teacher
before, never mind from Mr Finch.

'Well, don't let me keep you Mr Sparrow, good
job!'

Frankie flew off before Mr Finch changed his mind.

This was highly unusual. Sparrow school had ended for the day, but Frankie now had a busy night ahead of him. He was on his way to see his Uncle and fellow private investigator, Charlie.

Frankie flew as fast as he possibly could to the office where he worked with his Uncle. Uncle Charlie was a Private Investigator and Frankie now helped after school, at weekends and on school holidays. Frankie loved the job and he was very good at it. Together, the pair of them made a winning team.

'Frankie! About time you got here.' Charlie said as soon as Frankie entered. 'We've never been so busy! The phone's chirping away every two minutes and I've had so many birds asking for our help that I can't keep up.' Charlie was excited but looked incredibly stressed. His feathers were ruffled, and he fiddled with his bright green bow tie as he spoke.

'I'm here now Uncle, so no need to worry. What are we working on today?'

'That's the thing, I just don't know where to begin. I really don't. I've never had this problem before, we're too busy!'

Frankie moved over to a large and very messy pile of papers - his Uncle's case files. He lifted the top sheet.

'Cat terrorising birds?' Frankie said.

'Too dangerous.'

'Magpies terrorising humans?'

'Too dangerous.'

'Seagulls terrorising Magpies?'

'Too dangero- '

'Is there anything that's not too dangerous Uncle?' Frankie interrupted. 'Catching the magpie with Mrs Campbell's keys was just as dangerous as any of these cases.'

Charlie paced up and down. He wasn't used to being snowed under with work like he was now.

'What's this one here,' Frankie said, reading from a sheet of paper which Charlie had scrawled on. 'The Bird Stop Cafe might have to close?'

'Tell me more. I don't recall that file?' Charlie said, fiddling with his bow tie again.

'It says - Bird Stop Cafe to close, Fidget phoned. Is that Johnny Fidget?' Frankie said.

'Oh yes, I remember now. Johnny Fidget phoned. Frantic he was. Babbled on for ages! Said the trees which nest the Bird Stop Cafe are going to be demolished.'

'Demolished? That's terrible news.' Frankie said. 'We need to help.'

'What can we do though?'

'I'm not sure Uncle but I do know this... we've found our next case!'

CHAPTER 3

Time on their talons

Detective Doolan and his deputy, Detective Twittery, were perched above the pigeon police station watching the world go by. The rain had finally stopped, and it had turned into a lovely bright quiet day. *Too* quiet for the two police officers. The station was normally heaving with all kinds of birds reporting crimes but recently things had changed. These days, many birds had turned to private investigators to help them with their problems. The pigeon detectives had never had so much spare time on their talons. They knew things couldn't go on like this for much longer.

Detective Doolan had been installed as the pigeon police leader for a second term but confidence in his force was at an all-time low after it turned out that one of his own detectives had been responsible for half of the crime in his district. Disgraced former pigeon police detective Paulie Pratchett certainly had a lot to answer for. Thankfully, he had been stopped and was now serving time behind bars.

'We need to do something to regain everyone's trust - no one's reporting crime to us anymore because of that blasted Pratchett!' Detective Twittery said. Doolan knew she was right.

Most of the pigeon police were now left twiddling their talons with absolutely nothing to do. The owl parliament would soon intervene and replace the whole department if things didn't improve. Doolan and Twittery would be the first birds to be fired.

'I know.' Doolan said, scratching his head with his wing. 'I've been trying to think of ways we can sort it out, but I'm well and truly stumped.' The whole thing was stressing him out. 'If only we could solve a big case and show everyone we can be trusted.'

'Exactly' Twittery said. She too was thinking things over.

'There's no way we can do that if no one's reporting any crime to us though, is there?' Doolan said.

'Why don't we talk to Charlie and Frankie Sparrow? See if we can't help them out? I've heard they're struggling to cope.'

Doolan pondered this for a second and then smiled. 'Do you know something? I think that's a great idea.

Let's go and pay them a visit. See if we can help them out. If we show everyone we can solve their cases, the word will soon spread that the pigeon police are back on the ball.'

CHAPTER 4

Fidget and The Bird Stop Cafe

Johnny Fidget had sounded close to tears when Frankie had spoken to him on the phone to find out what was going on, so they had decided to meet up. Uncle Charlie and Frankie flew to meet him at the Bird Stop Cafe. Charlie still didn't think they could help but hoped he might be able to wangle a free meal out of it in any case.

Fidget was pacing up and down nervously when they arrived. Fidget was always pacing up and down no matter what was going on but today he was even more animated. Fidget was the most nervous and jumpy magpie the private investigators had ever encountered. Stevie Starling, the cafe owner, was trying to calm him down. He wasn't succeeding.

'Johnny, have a seat. Let's find out what's going on.' Uncle Charlie said.

'I can't sit,' Fidget said. 'I can't keep still, this is terrible!'

Charlie and Frankie sat down with Stevie. There were several bowls of food spread out on the table. Fidget continued to pace up and down.

'Can you tell us what's happened?' Charlie asked, eyeing up the food in front of him. His stomach growled.

'Stevie heard him! He says the trees will come down, simple as that. The only job I've ever had and now it's gone, finished, finito!' Fidget shouted, still pacing back and forth.

Stevie Starling told the sparrows what had happened. He gestured for the birds to help themselves to the food on the table in front of them, Charlie didn't need to be told twice.

'Yesterday morning, there was a van parked just below us on the grass and one of my customers told me he'd seen it a few times before in the same spot. So, I got to thinking 'what's this chap up to?' I wish I'd never found out.' Stevie said before being interrupted by Fidget.

'Crinklebottom developments! That's what it says on the van. They're going to knock us down to build houses for humans!'

'It might not come to that Johnny- 'Frankie said.

'-oh, it'll come to it alright. It's the curse, the Crinklebottom curse!" Fidget said.

Frankie and Charlie both looked at each other quizzically, Charlie even stopped eating for a second - The Crinklebottom curse?

'Johnny's got it into his head that there's some sort of curse around this Crinklebottom fella.' Stevie Starling explained.

'There is, I'm telling you! I've heard about it before-'

'Lot of nonsense if you ask me.' Stevie said, 'but one thing's for sure, this Crinklebottom chap is going to pull the trees down and he's going to do it soon.'

'Soon?' Fidget shouted. 'How soon?' This was worrying new information for Johnny. He paced up and down even faster now.

'If Crinklebottom has his way then this time next month the trees will be reduced to rubble.' Stevie said.

'How do you know that for sure?' Frankie said.

'Let me tell you...'

CHAPTER 5
Mr Crinklebottom

The dirty, once white, van came to a shuddering stop under the trees. Smoke billowed out from the exhaust and it made a loud clanging noise. The vehicle sounded as if it was on its last legs. Stevie Starling watched on from the trees above. This was undoubtedly the van that some of his customers had talked about in the cafe. He'd sat perched in the trees for over two hours waiting on it arriving and finally his patience had been rewarded.

The sign on the side of the van could just about be made out through all the grime, it read 'Crinklebottom Developments'. The door creaked open and out stepped a large man. He was smoking away at one of those horrible sticks that some of the older humans use. He was oddly dressed in a brown suit and large black wellington boots. Maybe he'd got dressed in the dark, Stevie thought. He had a mobile phone clamped to his ear and talked very loudly; he didn't seem to care who heard him. After all, there was no one around apart from the birds in the trees.

'Yes, yes. I know all of that - all I need to know now is when the demolition can take place and I can get on with making some more cash?' The man laughed, sending puffs of horrible smelling smoke into the trees above. Stevie tried his best not to choke. His eyes were burning!

'I don't care if the trees have stood there for hundreds of years.' The man shouted. 'I couldn't care less. Do you think wildlife and pesky birds are going to hold this up and stop me making more money?' Stevie watched on; the man puffed more horrible smoke into the air, Stevie couldn't help but cough this time.

'No, you listen to me! The trees will be down by the end of next month. Sooner, if I have my way. Who knows what little accident might occur! Then we can get on with building my flats.'

So, this was Mr Crinklebottom. What a thoroughly horrible chap Stevie thought to himself.

'Yes, I know that. Let me stop you there, has a little thing like planning permission ever stopped me before?' Crinklebottom laughed and then puffed up more horrible smoke. Stevie could hardly breathe.

'Nothing is going to stop Gerry Crinklebottom from making his fortune,' he said into the phone. 'By hook, or by crook, the trees are coming down and there coming down with or without your help!'

CHAPTER 6

The pigeons are here to help

The sign emblazoned on the door read 'Charlie & Frankie Sparrow: Private Investigator's', Detective Doolan tapped on it with his beak and entered.

'Where's young Frankie?' Doolan asked when he saw Charlie Sparrow was alone in the office. Doolan had been looking forward to hearing about Frankie's progress in becoming a fully-fledged private investigator.

'He's at school. He's got to keep up his education as well as help me to catch criminals! What can I do for you detective's?' Charlie said.

'Well, we were wondering if you needed some help.' Twittery said. 'Maybe we could take a small case or two off your talons?'

'Oh, I don't know about that.' Charlie said, smiling. Charlie had always wanted to work with the pigeon police but had never been allowed to join due to failing the entrance exams numerous times and now here was the leader and the deputy leader asking if they could help *him* out. Charlie had a thought; he could pass off some of the cases he felt were too dangerous to Doolan and Twittery. See if they could solve them without him or Frankie having to get involved and risk life and limb.

'I was just going to start on this case here.' Charlie said, smiling to himself. 'But since I'm a nice sparrow, I could let you guys have a go at solving it if you like?'

'What's the case?' Doolan said. He was that eager to help he would take anything Charlie could give him.

'Simple enough one to start with.' Charlie said, quickly grabbing the case file before the pigeons changed their minds. 'It's a small cat terror- annoying birds. Should be easy enough for the pigeon police to sort out.'

'Have you got any more?' Twittery asked.

'Well, if you insist, I could give you this one.'

Doolan opened the next file he had been given - Magpies terrorizing humans - he didn't like the sound of that one little bit but then again beggars couldn't be choosers, could they?

'We'll take them!' Twittery said. 'Once we've closed

these cases, we'll come back and help you out some more if you like?'

'Yeah, that would be great. Working in partnership with the pigeons is all I ever wanted. Plus, this case we're working on right now will take up most of our time. It's a puzzler.' Charlie said.

'What are you working on?' Doolan asked.

'It's the trees which nest the Bird Stop Cafe, some property developer is wanting to tear them down and he's not hanging about.'

'What's the property developer's name?' Twittery asked, fearing the answer.

'Crinkle…' Charlie consulted his file. 'Crinklebottom.'

'Have you heard of the Crinklebottom curse?' Twittery said.

'Mr Fidget mentioned something about that.'

'He's a bad egg is Crinklebottom.' Doolan said. 'We've had dealings with him before. I never believed in the curse, but I've seen it with my own eyes. You've got your work cut out.'

'What do you mean you've actually seen the curse?' Charlie said.

'We were working on saving trees before.' Doolan said. 'We thought we'd won as planning permission was denied and the humans are very big on planning permission. We thought that was it but then the next thing we know, there was some sort of freak accident and a huge truck crashed into the tree. Which meant they had to come down after all. Ended up Crinklebottom got his way and the trees were demolished. Shiny new houses were put in their place.'

'That's not really a curse though is it?' Charlie said. 'Sounds like an accident to me.'

'Ah, once maybe, but these things always seem to happen when Crinklebottom is concerned. Another time we were called in and again Crinklebottom was told trees couldn't come down. This time there was a huge flood and the trees were damaged and *again* he got his way.' Twittery said.

'Hmmm, that's just rotten bad luck. There's no way you could blame Crinklebottom for a flood.'

'It's the curse. I'm telling you Charlie.' Doolan said. 'Watch yourself with this one. He's a slippery customer is Mr Crinklebottom.'

At that there was a loud rumble of noise in the distance.

'What's that racket?' Charlie said.

The birds left Charlie's office to investigate.

CHAPTER 7

The diggers arrive

The noise which Charlie and the two pigeon detectives heard was almost deafening up close. Three large bulldozers had arrived at the trees which nested the Bird Stop Cafe. All the birds in the cafe had stopped eating and stared down in disbelief at the machines. Some of them tried to cover their ears from the din.

Mr Crinklebottom stood directly underneath the tree surveying the scene. He looked ridiculously pleased with himself. He was grinning from ear to ear and yet again he was puffing on one of his horrible sticks.

'Good, good, that's it.' He said quietly to himself. 'It's all coming together quite nicely.' Crinklebottom was delighted to see good progress being made. The sooner the trees came down, the sooner he would make more money.

Lots of birds had gathered in the trees to watch the

horrifying spectacle of the diggers lining up underneath their precious trees which housed many of their homes and businesses.

The demolition wasn't meant to be for ages thought Fidget, yet here was Crinklebottom and his workers looking ready for action.

'Oh no, this is terrible, it's begun already!' Fidget said. He fretted and then stressed some more but then a thought struck him, and he was more animated than ever. He flew off in a hurry.

'Calm down Johnny-' Stevie Starling said, before noticing Johnny Fidget had vanished.

'Right Hobbs, don't park that over there.' Crinklebottom gave his sidekick his orders. 'Move it here under this big old tree. This one will come down first I hope.'

However, the man called Hobbs just sat there in the cab and didn't move the large bulldozer.

'I can't move it Mr Crinklebottom, I can't start it.' Hobbs said. He was shaking.

'What do you mean you can't start it? Start the engine now!' Crinklebottom demanded.

'The keys… the keys are gone.' Hobbs said. He had gone very red in the face.

'What? Don't be so stupid! How can you have lost the keys?'

'I... I don't know what's happened.' Hobbs stuttered. 'They were here a minute ago.' He frantically searched for the keys.

'You literally just drove the diggers over here! Check your pockets!' Crinklebottom could not be dealing with incompetent workers. Not today. He flicked his horrible smoke stick onto the grass.

Hobbs checked his pockets but to no avail. There was no sign of any keys. How could this be? he thought. The keys had been right there in front of him and now they had vanished into thin air.

'This is ridiculous!' Crinklebottom shouted at Hobbs. 'Empty out your pockets!'

Poor Hobbs was forced to empty his pockets. Still there were no keys.

'Jump up and down. Maybe they've fallen through a hole in your pocket.' Crinklebottom said.

Hobbs looked ridiculous as he jumped up and down. He was doing star jumps. The birds watching on from the trees tried their best not to laugh too loud.

Charlie Sparrow and Detective's Doolan and Twittery had flown over for a closer look. They saw Mr Crinklebottom shouting at a small red-faced man wearing a yellow hard hat who was doing star jumps.

'What's going on?' Doolan asked Stevie Starling.

'It's Crinklebottom. He's getting everything ready

to take down the trees, even though the demolition isn't scheduled for weeks. It looks like his friend has lost the keys though! Look at his face, it's beetroot!' Stevie said with a laugh. At that Johnny Fidget reappeared. He was carrying something in his beak. Something shiny.

'Is that what I think it is Johnny?' Stevie asked.

'You know us magpies love shiny things!' Fidget laughed. He had stolen the keys from the digger. 'This will only stop them for a little while though. We need to come up with a plan to stop them once and for all.' All the assembled birds knew he was right.

CHAPTER 8

Pigeons problems

Charlie Sparrow really needed to organise his case files better. Detective Doolan stared down at the sheet in front of him which was headed 'Cat terrorizing birds'. Not 'small cat annoying birds' as Charlie had said. Doolan and Twittery both knew Charlie Sparrow had been eager to get both cases he'd given them off his talons. The detectives were just glad to have some work and hopefully, if all went well, they would have a lot more soon.

There wasn't much information to go on in Charlie's casefile, apart from the name of the cats owner, a Mrs Warburton, and the location of the house where the owner and cat both lived - the house under the trees which nested the wood pigeon school and the laundry.

Doolan and Twittery could have palmed the work

off to one of their team of officers but they had decided that they were going to handle both cases personally. They couldn't afford any slip ups if they were to salvage the pigeon police forces ailing reputation. Not that sorting out this cat, and then the magpies, would solve everything. However, it would be a start on the road to recovery. Former pigeon police detective Pratchett had left them with a mountain to climb after his terrible behaviour. The pigeon police were supposed to enforce the law, not break it as he had done on several occasions.

Doolan and Twittery had flown to the trees and perched right beside the laundry which was surprisingly quiet. Normally, birds of all shapes and sizes would be coming and going with large bags of washing. Doolan made a mental note to have a chat with the laundry owner and see what was going on. The wood pigeon school was also closed even though it wasn't the school holidays for a good while yet.

After only a few seconds of scanning the gardens below them, the two pigeons spotted the cat. They couldn't very well miss it. Both pigeon police officers looked at each other and sighed. 'Small cat' Charlie Sparrow had said. Either Charlie needed new glasses, or he was pulling their leg. They most certainly had their work cut out…

CHAPTER 9
Finch and Frankie's idea

'Are you okay, Frankie?' Mr Finch said. School had finished for the day, but Frankie had remained seated in his chair. He was deep in thought and had lost track of time. Normally, he was one of the first to fly away from school. Today, he was trying his hardest to come up with a plan which could save the trees and the Bird Stop cafe from demolition, but he was coming up short.

'It's this case I'm working on with my Uncle.' Frankie said. 'I can't think of a way to stop the trees being torn down.'

'Let me guess, it's a Mr Crinklebottom who wants to build on the land, isn't it?' Finch said.

'How did you know that?' Mr Finch certainly had Frankie's attention now.

'Normally, when trees are coming down it's

something to do with that ghastly man. He tore down the trees where my good friend Monty stayed last year.'

'That's terrible. My Uncle and I have taken on the case but it's harder work than we thought it would be.' Frankie said.

'If only there were some exotic birds or rare animals nesting in the trees.' Mr Finch laughed.

'What did you say Mr Finch?' Frankie said.

'I said, if only there were some exotic birds or rare animals nesting in the trees you're trying to save.'

'What good would that do if they are to be demolished?' Frankie said.

'Well, some birds and animals are known as protected species by the humans.' Mr Finch said. 'So, if there were any rare birds or animals in the trees then they wouldn't be *allowed* to tear them down. The humans have laws which would prevent it.'

'How do you know which birds and animals are protected?' Frankie asked, Mr Finch had certainly piqued his interest.

Mr Finch flew up and grabbed a book from one of his high bookshelves.

'Here we are.' Mr Finch flicked through the book until he came to the relevant page. 'Here's a full list.'

'Can I borrow this?' Frankie said, he was suddenly

very excited. Mr Finch had come up with an idea which might just work.

'Yes, of course.' Mr Finch said. 'I hope it helps!'

Frankie had a good feeling about this. This was the idea he had been searching for. He flew off quickly with the book under his wing.

CHAPTER 10

Cat close call

Doolan and Twittery had seen some big cats in their time but this feline was like nothing they had ever encountered. The cat was massive. Humungous!

'It's almost as big as a Tiger!' Detective Doolan said.

Detective Twittery wasn't in a mind to disagree. She didn't look too keen anymore. Doolan looked sick. He had turned a funny shade of pale.

The cat looked as fierce as a tiger as well. It certainly didn't look happy as it prowled up and down the garden. No wonder Charlie Sparrow was so eager to give them this case.

'Maybe we'd be best starting with the magpies terrorizing the humans? That might be easier than this.' Doolan said.

'No, we're here now. We'd best give it a go.' Twittery said. 'We can deal with the magpies after this.' She wasn't looking forward to either of the cases but there was no point putting it off, they needed to try and deal with the huge cat.

'Why don't we just try talking to the cat? ' Twittery said.

Detective Doolan didn't look too sure. 'Okay, I guess we can give it a shot.' Both birds moved along the branch which dangled into Mrs Warburton's garden. The large cat turned and looked up at the pigeon's progress. The birds held on to the branch and moved right to the edge.

'Excuse me, we were wondering if we could have a word. I'm Detective Doolan and this is Detective Twitt-'

The cat leapt and swiped at both pigeons. It took a handful of Doolan's feathers. Both birds flew up into the air to get away from the cats' sharp claws. There were leaves and feathers everywhere. Maybe talking to the cat wasn't the best idea after all. Doolan and Twittery flew over to the trees in the next garden and well out of reach from the angry cat. Doolan had looked in better shape, he had a chunk of feathers missing and was sweating profusely.

'That was a close one!' Doolan said, 'Maybe we'll need to come up with a plan B, I don't think this cat's the listening type.'

'You might be right.' Twittery said. 'Let's see if we have better luck with the magpies.'

Doolan remembered something before they left to tackle the magpie problem. He wanted to have a word with the owner of the laundry.

'Let's have a look in the laundry and see if they can help us out.' Doolan told Twittery.

Both birds flew the short distance and entered the laundry. It was deserted.

'Hello?' Twittery said. She was sure she could hear someone pottering about in the back.

A pair of chaffinches emerged from behind a curtain. 'How can we help you?' said the male chaffinch. He was a tiny little bird. Both birds had brightly coloured blue heads and predominantly red bodies with white markings. Both small chaffinches wore crisp white aprons.

'We were wondering if you could tell us anything about the cat in the house below?' Doolan said.

The small birds looked crestfallen. Claude and Cheryl Chaffinch had owned and run the laundry for years, but business had completely ground to a halt recently.

'Oh, you want to talk about the cat. I thought you might have some work for us. The cat has scared away our customers. No one wants to pick up or drop off laundry anymore with that beast on the loose.' Cheryl said.

'Have you tried reasoning with the cat?' Twittery said.

'I take it you have judging by the feathers your friend is missing.' Cheryl said, indicating the chunk of feathers absent on Detective Doolan's body.

Doolan looked a little embarrassed but quickly changed the subject with another question.

'What about the wood pigeon school, is it closed?' Doolan said.

'No point in them opening if the cat tries to get them any chance it gets. Two wood pigeons have been injured already.' Claude said.

Doolan and Twittery both knew they needed to stop the cat. It was causing chaos and misery for far too many birds. If they solved this problem, then it would help a lot of birds. Plus, word would spread that the pigeon police had saved the day.

One thing was for sure though: this wasn't going to be easy.

They needed a better plan.

CHAPTER 11

Pigeons progress

The pigeon police did have better luck with the magpies. After dealing with the furious cat, dealing with the magpies who had been 'terrorizing humans' turned out to be a walk in the park.

Doolan and Twittery didn't have to wait long until the magpies turned up and started causing problems for the humans below. They were whooping and laughing as they swooped down and stole food and other belongings from the humans who were trying to have a nice time in the park.

Doolan and Twittery had come up with a plan which could hopefully help both them and the private investigators. If they could get the magpies to stop terrorizing the good humans in the park that they currently were and instead get them to target Crinklebottom and his workers who were trying to demolish the trees, then everyone would be happy. Getting them to agree might be the sticking point.

Doolan and Twittery flew over to the trees from where the magpies were launching their attacks. Cautiously, they began to talk with them.

'Gentlemen! We have a little proposition for you.' Doolan shouted over. 'We know you have been causing problems for the humans.'

'Yeah and what about it?' the ringleader who was called Mitch said, he didn't look too friendly.

'Well, we'd like you to stop terrorizing these humans and start on another group. You can steal as much food and as many keys or belongings as you like, and the police will allow it to happen.' Twittery said.

This sounded very interesting for the magpies. They had assumed Doolan and Twittery were there to put an end to their fun, but the pigeons had offered them a way to get into mischief and not have the police come down on them.

'So, let me get this right, you want us to stop messing with one group of humans only to mess with another group? Is that right?' Mitch said. He didn't know whether to believe the pigeons or not. This seemed too good to be true. Mitch feared it could be some sort of trap.

'Exactly! We can all have some fun and it will help

a lot of birds out.' Doolan said. 'You'd actually be doing us a favour.'

'What do you want us to do?' Mitch said, smiling to the rest of his gang.

Detectives Doolan and Twittery gathered the magpies round and told them their plan.

CHAPTER 12

Rare plans

'What are you working on Frankie?' Charlie said. 'You've not stopped all morning.'

Frankie had been scribbling away furiously in his notepad for hours. If truth be told, he had been working most of the previous night as well. After he'd left school with Mr Finch's idea ringing in his ears he had got straight to work. Mr Finch had inadvertently given Frankie the idea which they could hopefully use to save the trees and in turn, The Bird Stop Cafe. He had compiled a list of the rare birds and animals which were found in Mr Finch's book. He was trying to think of anyone who might know some rare birds or animals but so far, he had drawn a blank. However, he was sure *someone* must know one of the animals or birds on the list.

'I've got it!' said Frankie, excitedly. 'This list here could save the trees!'

Charlie looked at him sceptically. 'What on earth are you talking about?'

'Mr Finch gave me the idea in school. He said if there were rare birds or animals in the trees then there would be no way the humans would tear them down. There are rules and laws preventing it!'

'I don't see how this helps us Frankie.' Charlie said. 'There's no rare birds or animals in the trees?'

'At the moment there's no rare birds or animals in the trees, you mean!' Frankie held up the list he had prepared. 'This here will help us. Between us all we must know at least one bird or animal which falls into this rare or protected species category. Then, it's just a matter of getting them to come and stay in the trees.'

'Hmmmm, interesting idea Frankie, but how are we going to let the humans know that there are now protected animals in the trees? They could demolish them before they even see these rare species.'

Frankie hadn't thought about this, but he was sure they could find a way around it.

'We'll work it out.' Frankie said. 'Don't worry Uncle.'

'We'll see.' Charlie said. 'You can present this at the Owl Parliament meeting tonight and we'll see what they say. At least it's the start of a good idea. Well done Frankie!'

CHAPTER 13
Crinklebottom's visit

Frankie Sparrow had just left the Bird Stop Cafe and was now perched in the trees taking in his surroundings. He was trying to work out how his plan would come to fruition. He was thinking about what he would say at the Owl Parliament meeting which was to take place later that night. Where would the rare birds or animals go which would maximise the chances of them being seen by any humans on the ground?

He had been perched on a branch deep in thought when the noise of a vehicle brought him back to life. It was the dirty white van. Mr Crinklebottom was back.

He exited his van and moved over to the tree which Frankie was perched in. He looked up into the trees. He couldn't see Frankie through all the branches and leaves but Frankie had clear sight of him.

Mr Crinklebottom had brought spare keys for the diggers. He couldn't trust Hobbs to do anything right.

Crinklebottom knew the previous keys hadn't just vanished without a trace. Maybe birds had stolen them he thought or maybe Hobbs was the most incompetent man he'd ever come across in his life. Yes, that was probably it. Hobbs couldn't be trusted to do anything right. Crinklebottom often wondered why he kept him around. After this project was finished, he would make sure and fire the man. He'd put up with him for far too long.

Crinklebottom squinted up into the trees. He thought he could spot a bird's nest halfway up the tree. It was a strange place for a nest as it was reasonably low down. The nest hadn't been there any time he'd checked before. He would have noticed it. He needed less birds nesting in the trees, not more of the horrible creatures. He picked up a rock and threw it at the nest. Nothing happened. The rock just bounced away and narrowly missed whacking him on the head. He decided climbing the tree would be a better idea.

He started to climb the tree so as he could get a closer look. Unknown to Crinklebottom, the birds had foreseen that someone might want to climb the trees and get to them. They had used a mixture of water and oil to coat certain parts of the tree bark and make it nice and slippery for anyone silly enough to climb it.

Crinklebottom started his ascent. For a big man he was making good progress. Frankie saw him making his way up the tree. He quickly flew down and turned on the shower in the lower shower room and changed its position which sent a stream of rainwater sliding down the bark. The water mixed in with the oil and reached the ascending Crinklebottom. He tried his best to hold on, but he knew he was losing his grip. His legs and arms were flailing, trying to find some more purchase on the tree. It was a hopeless task. The water continued to come down the bark and as it mixed with the thin layer of oil it meant no one could hold on. Crinklebottom didn't stand a chance.

"Aaaaaaaaarghhhh!!" Crinklebottom shouted as he lost his grip. He fell ten feet or so back to the ground below with a loud crash. He sat at the bottom of the tree seeing stars. His suit was ruined because of the mud and grass stains, plus there was now a large rip which had exposed his bright red underpants. He also had a large bump on the top of his head from where he had fallen.

Crinklebottom was furious. However, he was glad that no one was around to witness what had happened. The embarrassment would have been too much. Crinklebottom stood, then angrily kicked the tree, which only resulted in him hurting his toes. He let out an angry scream and then limped back to the van holding his sore head with one hand and covering his bright red underpants with the other.

Frankie was laughing at Crinklebottom and his brightly coloured underpants. He was glad he had been around to see what had happened. He made a note to himself, he had to get around the clock surveillance on the trees. What would happen if Crinklebottom came back when there was no one around?

CHAPTER 14

Ding ding, round two

Detective's Doolan and Twittery were back for round two with the massive cat who was still causing all sorts of problems for any bird unfortunate enough to be in the vicinity of the gardens. Their first meeting had not gone at all well. They knew they had to come back with different ideas and tactics. They needed to stop the cat; he was causing too much disruption. The chaffinch's laundry was deserted, and the wood pigeon school remained closed. All because of the cat.

This time they had returned with back up. They had brought along four pigeon police colleagues *and* a large net. The plan was simple enough. They were to catch the cat in the net, calm it down and then talk things through. They were going to try and come to some sort of arrangement which would allow the birds to go about their daily business without fear of being eaten or attacked by the huge cat. Well, that was the plan, but as you know, even best laid plans can go wrong.

The cat was strolling about the garden, looking into the sky and the trees for any bird who would become easy prey. Detective Doolan flew to one side of the garden, Detective Twittery flew to the other side. The cat hissed and eyed them both with suspicion. The four pigeon police officers with the large net remained hidden in the trees. Doolan had told them to wait for his signal.

He hovered down until he was close enough for the cat to strike. The cat moved towards him menacingly.

Doolan started flapping his wings about manically, this was the signal the rest of the birds had been waiting for. On cue, Twittery flew down and started flapping her wings. The cat didn't know which pigeon to go for first.

The four pigeons emerged from the trees and swooped down holding the net wide. The cat was distracted wondering what Doolan and Twittery were up to. It didn't see the pigeons flying behind him. They scooped him up in the huge net. The cat was captured! The birds lifted the cat off the ground in the net and that is where things started to go pear shaped. The cat was too heavy! It was thrashing around and slashing at the net. The pigeons couldn't hold the net in the air. They were being dragged back down to the ground. The cat wildly slashed at the net with large sharp claws! There was a small tear in the fabric and then a large ripping noise. The net was destroyed, and the cat was free again. All the pigeons scattered into the air as the cat lunged at them. It looked livid now. The pigeons flew high into the trees and tried to think through their next move. The cat had evaded them once again. The net was ruined, and the pigeons were no further forward. No wonder Charlie Sparrow hadn't wanted anything to do with this case.

What were they going to do now?

CHAPTER 15
Owl Parliament meeting

There were birds of all different shapes, sizes and colours gathered in the Owl Parliament. It was a magnificent sight. The parliament was lit up with lots of small candles as all meetings normally took place at night-time. The owls you see worked strange hours and slept for most of the day.

It was in all the bird's interests to keep The Bird Stop Cafe open as most, if not all of them, had eaten there at one point or another, so a sizeable crowd had gathered at the parliament for the meeting.

Peggy Beans brought the meeting of the Owl Parliament to order. She was the oldest and wisest owl there was and the leader of the parliament.

'Good evening. Thanks everyone for coming along tonight. As you no doubt know, we have a problem and it involves our old friend Mr Crinklebottom.'

There were a few moans and groans from the assembled birds. Many had heard of, or dealt with, Mr Crinklebottom before and they knew his name spelt trouble.

'Mr Crinklebottom is going to tear down the large group of trees which nest, among other things, The Bird Stop Cafe. Now, we all know this can't be allowed to happen. So, I've called this meeting to try and talk through the problem and hopefully between us all we can come up with some sort of strategy and save the trees.'

'Peggy!' Charlie Sparrow shouted. 'Frankie has an idea that might just help!' He had discussed things further with his nephew and he was now convinced the plan would work. All the birds turned to look at Charlie, or more specifically at Frankie who was perched beside him. Charlie pushed him forward to speak. Frankie's cheeks had gone bright red.

'Let's hear it young sparrow.' Peggy Beans said. 'The floor is all yours.'

Frankie had been thrust into the spotlight. He stood to address the large number of birds at the meeting.

'Good evening everyone,' Frankie said. 'Mr Crinklebottom must have planning permission to rip down our precious trees.' All the birds knew this, they didn't look impressed. Frankie nervously continued.

'However, if there are rare animals or birds in the trees then planning permission would be rejected by the humans and the demolition would have to stop.' He had their attention now.

Frankie held papers up into the air. 'I've compiled this list here which will help us. The rare birds or animals are known as a protected species. They include badgers and bats, otters and red squirrels and natterjack toads. The list of protected birds includes eagles and ospreys, snowy owls and peregrine's, buzzards and kingfishers.'

'Did you say snowy owls are protected?' Peggy Beans said.

Frankie looked at the list again to make sure. 'Yes. Snowy owls are protected.'

'Well, why didn't you say?' Peggy said, with a huge grin on her face. 'My cousins are snowy owls!'

'That's great news!' Charlie Sparrow shouted.

'The only thing is though; they stay over 200 miles away.' Peggy said.

'I could fly them here!' Miles shouted. He was a huge seagull who worked at the airport as a pilot.

'There's too many of them just for you Miles.' Peggy said. 'And they don't travel light!'

'There's lots of us pilots you know, they'd love to lend a claw.' Miles said.

'That would be a super help Miles, it's great how we can all pull together in times of crisis like this.' Peggy said.

It was sorted. They had the start of a viable plan at least. Everyone seemed a bit happier now, apart from Johnny Fidget. He was still fretting.

'Rare birds? That's what we're relying on? It's not going to work. Only job I've ever had and now it's gone. Finished. Done and dusted. May as well just pull the trees down and be done with it.' Fidget said.

'Good to see your being optimistic Johnny.' Stevie Starling laughed. 'At least we have a shot at saving the cafe now. C'mon, let's think positive, this might just work.'

Most of the birds had been filled with some much-needed hope that the trees could now be saved. The brief meeting was ending on a high note... that was until one of the Owl Parliament stood, squinted into the distance and said:

'Is that smoke I can see coming from the trees?'

CHAPTER 16
Crinklebottom curse strikes

Mr Crinklebottom had been gazing up at the trees for a considerable period of time. He finished another one of his horrible smoke sticks but instead of throwing this one away onto the grass, like he usually did, he paused. He returned to his van and came back with a green container which had a black spout. Frankie Sparrow had asked his friend Jeff Robin to keep a look out whilst everyone else was at the Owl Parliament meeting. Jeff was a tiny little robin red breast and wouldn't be seen by anyone. He had been trying not to choke from all the disgusting smoke which Crinklebottom was sending skywards from his smoke sticks. Now, he looked on from the trees with concern. What on earth was he up to? Jeff thought. What was in the green container? Whatever it was, Jeff didn't think it was good news.

Crinklebottom poured some clear liquid from the container around the trunk of the tree. He was acting very suspiciously. Then Jeff could smell the liquid. It was petrol! Crinklebottom was pouring petrol around the trunk of the tree! Crinklebottom then pressed the still burning smoke stick against some papers and immediately they set alight. Jeff was really worried now. Crinklebottom placed the burning papers under the tree directly in front of him. The tree which was surrounded by petrol! Highly flammable petrol! The flames immediately took hold. Jeff Robin couldn't believe his eyes. Mr Crinklebottom smiled to himself and then quickly moved back towards his van. Leaning against the driver's door, he spoke into his phone. Jeff could hear every word.

'The trees will be down a bit quicker than we'd thought Hobbs. Don't ask silly questions. Just get the team ready to move all the debris tomorrow. Let's just say, the Crinklebottom curse has struck again!' he laughed as he hung up the phone.

Crinklebottom jumped in his van, started the engine and sped away. He looked in his rear-view mirror at the flames which were starting to climb up the tree. He hoped the fire would spread to the other trees. He hoped they would all be burnt to a cinder. Crinklebottom had just accelerated his plans. There would be no more delays. Nothing would stop him now. Finally, the trees would be gone, and he could get on with making some lovely cash.

Jeff Robin had watched the events with horror. He had listened to Crinklebottom laughing on his phone. 'The Crinklebottom curse has struck again.' That's what he had shouted into his phone with glee.

Jeff needed to do something to stop this.

He needed to act fast.

CHAPTER 17
Sound the alarm!

A worrying amount of smoke was rising into the trees. Jeff Robin coughed as it threatened to engulf him. He couldn't believe what had just happened. How could someone start a fire like that and just run off? He watched as Mr Crinklebottom drove away in his old van and then got straight to work. He knew this wasn't looking good. It was a good job Frankie had asked him to watch the trees. If he didn't act quickly, then the fire would destroy everything. There was no doubt in his mind about that.

'Sound the emergency alarm!' Jeff shouted. However, no one was there. All the birds who would normally be in the trees were at the Owl Parliament meeting. He was talking to himself!

Jeff knew that this was his chance to shine. He needed to save the day.

He flew as fast as he could and found the alarm. It was a large red lever with CAUTION written in huge letters above it. It was seldom used. The lever was only to be pulled in great emergencies. If this wasn't a great emergency, then what was Jeff thought. He pulled on the lever with all his might and eventually it released. A screeching high-pitched noise sounded. The sound of the alarm would alert any birds within a mile of the trees.

Jeff then quickly flew to all the different nests located within the trees and started to peck on doors with his beak. He was sure that everyone was at the Owl Parliament meeting but he had to be certain that no one was left behind. He couldn't take any risks, not when it came to a fire like this – birds' lives could be at stake. Thankfully no one seemed to be at home.

Jeff swooped to the nest below The Bird Stop Cafe which he knew housed a shower room. He turned on the four showers so as the water would help fight the incoming fire. A steady stream of water was now falling onto the flames below, but it didn't seem to be making much of a difference. He could feel the intense heat rising.

Jeff knew that help would be on the way, birds would come flying as soon as they heard the alarm.

He just hoped they wouldn't be too late…

CHAPTER 18

FIRE!

Jeff was relieved when help started to arrive. He had done all he could to try and stop the fire from spreading. However, the smoke was almost overpowering, and the flames were still glowing at the bottom of the trees. The birds needed to act quickly to save the trees.

Thankfully, Jeff had made sure that no birds had been left behind in their nests so no one would be hurt. Yet, if they didn't get their act together quickly the trees would be reduced to ashes and Crinklebottom would have succeeded in his mission to tear them down.

The birds who had been assembled at the Owl Parliament had all made their way towards the smoke. They had heard the alarm seconds after the smoke had been spotted.

'Anyone with keys, get to your nests and turn on your showers and taps, use the diverter to make sure all the water comes down to fight the fire.' Charlie Sparrow said. He was taking it upon himself to organise everyone as Peggy Beans was still making her way from the parliament. She wasn't as fast as she used to be.

'Miles - you and the larger birds, fill as many emergency buckets with water as you can and throw them down to dampen the flames. Get to it!' Charlie said.

'Everyone else, split into two groups - first group will be you lot over here, I want you to fill water into any container you can. The second group - I want you making as much noise to alert the humans below, if some humans with their hoses help then the fire won't stand a chance. Together we can save the trees. Let's go!' Frankie was impressed with his Uncle. Charlie had really stepped up.

Everyone flew into action. Teamwork was the order of the day. The fire was still blazing at the foot of the trees but already the water from the showers had started to dampen any flames which were threatening to rise. Miles and seven more huge seagulls flew back and forth with buckets laden with water which they tipped onto the flames. It was working. They had managed to get the fire under some sort of control.

A couple of humans had been alerted by the racket the birds were making and had started using garden hoses at the bottom of the trees. Everyone really was working together. The fire was almost out, and the trees had been saved.

'It was Crinklebottom!' Jeff Robin said, when he saw Frankie.

'I had a feeling he might try something.' Frankie said. 'It's a good job you were here to see him. It looks like you've saved the day.' Jeff's feathers had been turned dark grey due to the smoke, the red feathers on his chest were barely visible.

'I heard him on his phone, he said 'The Crinklebottom curse had struck again!' He set our trees on fire and he was laughing about it. Laughing!' Jeff coughed as he spoke. He couldn't believe what had happened. What he had witnessed. How could anyone act like that? Crinklebottom could have killed them all and he didn't seem to care one little bit.

Frankie was right, Jeff Robin's quick thinking *had* saved the day. The flames were completely extinguished now and not one nest had been damaged. The smell of smoke was strong but that would dissipate over the coming days.

Crinklebottom and his 'curse' had been defeated,

for now. The birds all knew that it wasn't over yet. They had to make sure Crinklebottom was stopped once and for all.

CHAPTER 19

Crinklebottom curses

Mr Crinklebottom arrived at the trees the next morning. He leapt down from his van in shock. He couldn't believe his eyes. He didn't know what had happened. He had expected all the trees to be turned into a pile of rubble and ashes but there was only a minimal amount of damage. What was going on? The fire had been well underway when he made his hasty exit from the scene. Now, if it wasn't for the smell of smoke and a few black scorch marks on the tree bark, you'd never know there had been a fire raging here last night. A fire which he himself had started.

Crinklebottom was furious. His best laid plans had been scuppered yet again. How could this have happened? These trees were supposed to be burnt to rubble! The Crinklebottom curse was supposed to have struck again. How could this be?

First, the keys had gone missing from his diggers. Then, he'd heard the birds laughing at him when he fell from the tree as he was trying to destroy the nest and now, the fire which he had started had somehow been put out. Was he going mad?

Mr Crinklebottom was stressed out. No one was telling him what he wanted to hear and still the trees hadn't been pulled down. He swore that the trees were laughing at him. Or, at least, the birds within the trees were laughing at him. Maybe he really was slowing losing his marbles. He pulled another horrible smoking stick from his pocket and fumbled with it until it was lit; stinking smoke began to rise again.

Crinklebottom looked up into the trees as he puffed away. Unfortunately for him he looked up just as Miles was trying to balance some of the excess water which they hadn't needed to put out the fire. Miles always had been a little clumsy. He staggered from one side of the tree to the next and the large basin of water which was finely balanced on his back slipped. The basin flipped upside down, caught on a branch and emptied all the water onto the hapless person stood below... Mr Crinklebottom. He was well and truly soaked. The horrible smoking stick in his mouth had been extinguished.

Hobbs looked horrified. The rest of the workers

tried not to laugh out loud. The sound of birds chirping together in the trees was loud and clear. Crinklebottom stormed away in a huff, Hobbs followed on. Crinklebottom squelched his way back into his van and slapped his hands down on the steering wheel. He screamed with rage. He punched the steering wheel as hard as he could which only succeeded in hurting his knuckles. He tightly closed his eyes and tried to think. Tried to compose himself. 'Tomorrow is another day, the trees will come down tomorrow.' he said to himself. Hobbs stood outside the van not knowing what to do. Crinklebottom started the engine which sent a plume of black smoke into the air and drove away, narrowly missing the hapless Hobbs.

The trees wouldn't be getting torn down today.

CHAPTER 20
Pigeons and the Gadget

Doolan and Twittery had to come up with a better plan to tackle the huge cat. If the two detectives continued the way they were going they would end up a laughing stock or worse, they would end up as lunch for the cat.

They were having a meeting with Swifty the Gadget who was sure to have something which could help them. Swifty himself had been injured by a cat some years before and now had to come up with all sorts of imaginative ways to keep himself safe as he could only fly a very limited distance and walked with a stick.

'Detective's, what a nice surprise. How can I help you today?' Swifty said as the two pigeons entered his home which doubled as his office.

'We need your help with a little problem. Well, a big problem actually. It's to do with a cat.' Detective Twittery said.

'A cat? That doesn't narrow it down. Most of the problems I deal with nowadays seem to involve cats. Which one?'

'Do you know Mrs Warburton's cat?' Doolan said.

'Unfortunately, yes, yes I do.' Swifty shuddered. He'd had a few run ins with the very same cat.

'We were wondering if there was anything you could give us to help?' Twittery said.

'Oh, I'm sure I'll have something.' Swifty the Gadget went to work, looking through his cupboards and workspace for something which would help the pigeons.

'Now, let me see. This machine I'm going to give you, it's not been fully tested yet, but the initial signs are very pleasing. Very pleasing indeed. I call this the 'Swifty exaggerator'.'

Both pigeons waited patiently for Swifty to show them what the contraption he was holding could do. Swifty the Gadget was always coming up with all sorts of weird and wonderful inventions.

'Now, the main thing about the Warburton cat - whose real name is Pebbles by the way - is the sheer size of the beast. Now, what if *you* were to appear bigger than the cat?' Swifty said.

The pigeons were perplexed 'bigger than the cat'? How was that even possible? And the huge cat was named Pebbles? The pigeons tried not to laugh. The cat certainly didn't look like a Pebbles.

'Okay, this is how it works,' Swifty said. 'Detective Doolan can you hold the machine and point it towards me, then press the large red button.'

Doolan did as he was told. Immediately the machine whirred into life. Swifty, who was only a tiny little bird, appeared in front of them and he was enormous! The pigeons both took a step back.

'Amazing isn't it!' Swifty's voice was louder than ever. 'I'm still working out some of the kinks, but I think this should help you with Pebbles. What do you think?'

Both pigeons looked at each other and smiled. This might just work.

CHAPTER 21

Incoming owls at the airport

Charlie, Frankie, Johnny Fidget and Peggy Beans had been waiting at the airport for over an hour.

'There not coming.' Johnny Fidget said as he paced up and down. 'Something's gone wrong. I can feel it. I knew it was all too good to be true.'

The rest of the birds tried not to show how anxious they were. Miles and his friends *should* have been there by now. 'Just when you think there's a small chance of the trees being saved; everything gets ruined all over again-'

As Fidget rambled on, he was interrupted by the wonderful sound of five of the largest seagulls your ever likely to see appearing on the horizon. Miles triumphantly led the group. They carried the snowy owls and masses of luggage. The seagulls whooshed down and made a less than safe landing. It was a good job all the owl's belongings and the owl's themselves had been tied down.

'Took us longer than we imagined but we made it in the end.' Miles said after he had eventually landed on firm ground. The snowy owls looked terrified as they disembarked from their flight.

'Mildred! It's great you're here,' Peggy said. 'We're delighted to see you!' Her cousin Mildred did not look best pleased.

'Never in my life have I been so scared. This one should never be allowed to fly passengers - he's out of control!' Mildred said, adjusting her feathers. 'How did he ever get his pilot's license?' Mildred shouted. Miles looked a little sheepish.

'It was a bit of a bumpy flight.' Miles explained, as he moved off to refuel with some much-needed food.

'And as for his eating, the gull never stops, he eats when he's flying! I've never seen anything like it.' Mildred said.

'You're here safe and sound and that's all that matters. Great that you could help us out like this.' Peggy said. 'All of us are so pleased you could help us with our little predicament.' Peggy indicated for the other birds to come over. After she had made introductions, the four snowy owls assembled.

'We'd appreciate it if you could show us to our

accommodation Peggy.' Mildred said. 'We are absolutely exhausted after our treacherous travels.'

'No problem. Follow me. Miles and the others will follow on with all of your bags.' Peggy said. They certainly had a lot of luggage.

'We'll let you get settled and then discuss our plans tonight. We really are delighted you could come.' Peggy Beans said. Mildred and the rest of the owls didn't look delighted to be there. It would take them some time for them to calm down after their turbulent flight. Unfortunately, time was something none of the birds had…

CHAPTER 22

The magpies

The sun was shining bright in the sky. The birds were singing happily in the trees and all was right with the world. That was until Mr Crinklebottom and the workmen turned up. They were back sooner than anyone had anticipated. Crinklebottom was running the show. He was acting as if nothing had happened even though the smell of smoke still lingered. He was issuing instructions to Hobbs, who in turn was directing the rest of the workforce.

Stevie Starling had been told to alert Charlie or Frankie Sparrow should anything happen with regards to the trees when they weren't there. Stevie phoned Charlie. Charlie in turn alerted Detective Doolan. Doolan flew into action and both he and Detective Twittery arrived with a gang of magpies in tow. The magpies were excited and cawed at each other loudly.

The birds who had been singing in the trees just moments before were silent now. They had no idea what was happening but watched on with keen interest.

Doolan told Stevie that they had managed to come to an agreement with the magpies. He told him that they were here to help. If the magpies enjoyed terrorizing humans so much, then why not terrorise Mr Crinklebottom and his cronies who were so eager to pull down the trees. At this point Stevie would take help from anyone if it helped save his business.

The magpies flew into action with relish.

They stole keys.

They grabbed hard hats.

They flew into the digger's cabs.

There was bird poo flying everywhere.

The workmen hadn't signed up for this. Some of them were covered in bird poo and others were being pecked by the magpies. They'd had enough and scattered everywhere. They weren't sticking around to do any work with all of this going on. Mr Crinklebottom was furious.

'Where are you going?' Crinklebottom shouted. 'It's just a few magpies!' However, his words were falling on deaf ears, the workers were off. With the workers fleeing, the magpies turned their attentions to the rogue property developer. When Crinklebottom spotted the magpies were now after him he started to run. He was flapping his arms wildly as he tried to escape the black and white feathered birds.

'Hobbs!' Crinklebottom shouted. 'Help me Hobbs!'

'I'm coming boss!' Hobbs said, giving chase. Hobbs had grabbed a large sweeping brush and was whacking it back and forth at the magpies. The birds flew into the air, but Hobbs had closed his eyes. He swung blindly back and forth with the brush and whacked Mr Crinklebottom right on the side of the head. Crinklebottom fell backwards onto the ground and screamed at the hapless Hobbs who had eventually opened his eyes.

'Sorry boss.' Hobbs said.

Crinklebottom angrily grabbed the brush from Hobbs and started chasing him with it. Hobbs was doing the running this time! The birds in the trees laughed as they watched the comical scene play out in front of them. Hobbs ran behind one of the trees. He was trying to hide from his horrible boss. Detective's Doolan and Twittery had seen enough. They both flew down from the tree. They were carrying a large branch. As Crinklebottom ran towards the tree where Hobbs was hiding, the two pigeons raised the branch just a touch off the ground. Crinklebottom was in a rage and only had eyes for Hobbs. He didn't see the branch which the pigeons were using as a tripwire. He ran and his foot made contact with the branch. There was no stopping his fall. He stumbled forward. He had lost control and came to a crashing halt in a muddy puddle under the tree which Hobbs now appeared from.

'Are you okay boss?' Hobbs asked quietly.

'Okay?' Crinklebottom said. 'Do I look okay? I've had just about enough of you Hobbs. Get out of my sight!'

Hobbs didn't need to be told twice. He scurried away from his boss.

Crinklebottom lay in the muddy puddle at the bottom of tree. He was absolutely fuming. He mumbled to himself as he picked himself up from the puddle. Unfortunately for him he got up just as a bird dropping fell from above and splatted right onto his shoulder. He had now turned bright red with rage. Crinklebottom screamed up at the trees in frustration. Why was nothing going right? Why was this happening to him?

CHAPTER 23

Snowy owls

The snowy owls had settled in well. Or, as well as anyone could have expected them to. Frankie's father, Harry Sparrow, had been drafted in to alter two of the nests in the soon to be demolished trees so as the owls felt at home. Harry knew that the snowy owls were very pampered and notoriously hard to please. He was glad that their complaints had been kept to a minimum so far. Frankie's father ran Harry's Homes, they were the best nestbuider's around and they had done outstanding work in building a large extension to the nests and refurbishing the two properties in such a short period of time. The owls had so much luggage that some of their bags had to be kept in a third nest! All in all, Harry and his team had worked wonders and he was sure that the nests were fit for a King never mind a group of pampered snowy owls.

The main problem Harry had encountered apart from the lack of storage space was the faint smell of smoke which still lingered in the trees after Crinklebottom's fire. To combat this, Harry had placed some nice smelling salts in the lining of the nest walls which were to be used by the snowy owls. He really had gone the extra mile.

After all the disruption and the trouble everyone had endured to make the owls feel so welcome it was imperative that the plan worked, and the trees were saved.

The snowy owls had eaten a nice meal which had been prepared by Stevie and his staff at the café. Now they were resting. They had only been sleeping for an hour or two after their long and treacherous flight. Loud snoring could be heard from within the nest. Mildred had told Peggy not to disturb them under any circumstances. She had been adamant that they all needed time to recover. However, time was running out in the quest to save the trees. The plan would have to be set in motion imminently, if the owls agreed that was. Peggy wasn't looking forward to waking them up but there was no time to wait.

Frankie and Charlie had come up with an idea which they hoped would work. They had informed Peggy Beans and now the three of them were hovering outside the snowy owl's nest. The owls would be furious at having their rest interrupted, but the fate of the trees depended on the plan being put into action. They simply couldn't wait any longer. Without delay, Peggy Beans pecked on the nest door…

CHAPTER 24

Peggy Beans

'What is the meaning of this! What in Percy Pigeons name is going on?' Mildred said. Her feathers were dishevelled, and she looked furious that her sleep had been so rudely interrupted.

'I'm sorry Mildred but this can't wait,' Peggy said. 'We need to start right now with the plan. I promise, if things go well then you can all rest and no one will bother you again.'

'Never in my life have I-' Mildred said, Peggy cut her off, there was no time for any of this.

'You need to make yourselves known to the humans around here and we must start right away. I want all of you to fly into the gardens of the humans below. Let them see you, let them get a right good look at you. Let them see you fly into the trees, so they know without any shadow of a doubt that you are staying in these trees.' Peggy said.

'Well I never… this goes against everything I've ever learned or taught in my life.' Mildred said. 'If you insist then we will do it, but I'm not pleased about this. Not pleased at all. If anything happens to any of us, then on your head be it Peggy Beans. On your head be it!'

'The last thing we want is for anything to happen to you.' Peggy said. 'We'll have birds watching out for you to make sure you're all safe. Mildred, we can't thank you enough, but we need this to happen as soon as possible.'

'Okay, we will help. That's why we're here after all but let it be known Peggy Beans, let it be known that I am not happy about this at all!'

'Thank you, Mildred. Your objections have been noted. Now, if you could all go with Frankie and Charlie here, they will show you where to go.'

Frankie and Charlie showed the owls where they needed to perch which would give them the best chance of being spotted. The snowy owls would take it in shifts to fly down into the surrounding gardens which, all going well, would alert the humans to their presence. Whether or not the humans would then call in the relevant authorities was in the lap of the Gods.

CHAPTER 25

Hobbs keeps quiet

Hobbs was scared trying to have a conversation with Mr Crinklebottom at the best of times but today he really was terrified. He didn't think he'd even be able to get the words out properly. Hobbs had been told by one of the workmen and then by a little old lady who lived in one of the nearby houses that they had spotted owls in the trees. The very trees which Hobbs and the rest of them had been instructed to take down. The ones which Mr Crinklebottom was *demanding* they take down sooner than planned. He'd heard rumours that Mr Crinklebottom was the one who had started the fire which nearly destroyed the trees but surely not even *he* could be that callous or flout the health and safety laws so much. Although, on the phone he had said that the Crinklebottom curse had struck again. No, not even Mr Crinklebottom would stoop so low.

Hobbs knew he had to tell his boss that rare owls had been spotted in and around the trees. He knew this news wouldn't be taken kindly. Hobbs also knew that he'd probably be given the blame. Everything that had gone wrong was down to him it seemed, whereas anything that went right was down to Mr Crinklebottom. Hobbs even seemed to have been given the blame for the episode with all the magpies attacking the workers and Crinklebottom. How on earth could he have been responsible for that?

Hobbs spotted Mr Crinklebottom. He looked like he was in a foul mood.

'Mr Crinklebottom?' Hobbs said.

'What is it Hobbs?' Crinklebottom replied. He really did not seem happy at all.

'Err, it's just I-' Hobbs was stumbling over his words. His boss seemed to have that effect on him.

'Spit it out. What is it?'

'Err, nothing, it's nothing. I was just wondering how you were feeling today?'

Hobbs couldn't bring himself to upset Crinklebottom anymore.

'I'd be feeling a hell of a lot better if I didn't have to stand listening to you and I'd be delighted if these blasted trees fell to the ground!'

So, in the end Hobbs didn't tell Mr Crinklebottom about the owls being spotted in the trees.

CHAPTER 26

Pigeons victorious

Doolan and Twittery were poised in the trees. They were waiting on Mrs Warburton's cat. Pebbles. The detectives still couldn't believe the cat was named Pebbles. They had brought along the 'Swifty exaggerator' which they planned to use as soon as they spotted the large beast.

After around twenty minutes of nervous waiting, Pebbles appeared.

'Right, no time like the present. Let's do this.' Doolan said. 'Wait until I'm in position, then press the red button.' He hoped this worked. If it didn't then he would have to get out of there quick smart.

Doolan hovered down into the garden. Twittery waited until the very last moment and then pressed the button.

Immediately Detective Doolan blew up in size or

so it appeared. He was enormous! Swifty's machine was working. Doolan made his way over to Pebbles who was now snoozing at the bottom of the garden.

'PEBBLE'S!' Doolan bellowed, his voice almost deafening the cat.

"What's all the noise? What's going on? Is it feeding time already?' Pebbles said, was she still dreaming? The large cat opened her eyes and then stumbled backwards when she saw the huge pigeon in front of her.

'Pebble's we need to talk. *THIS CAN'T GO ON!* You can't keep terrorizing birds in this garden. It needs to stop, and it needs to stop *NOW! DO YOU HEAR ME?*' Doolan said, his voice still louder than any pigeons had ever been.

Pebble's couldn't believe her eyes or ears. This looked like the same pigeon police officer she had chased out the garden a few days ago but now he was huge! He was ten times the size of a normal pigeon. And his voice was so loud it was hurting her ears. What was happening?

'DO YOU UNDERSTAND ME PEBBLES!?!' Doolan boomed.

'Ye… yes I understand. Just don't hurt me! Please!' Pebbles stuttered. She wasn't used to anyone telling her what to do but she'd never seen a bird so big and fierce before. She'd never heard a bird be so loud before.

'I want you to apologise to any birds you have hurt in the past and I want you to be as good as gold going forward. No more chasing, attacking, hitting or terrifying anyone. And in return we will leave you to go about your business. However, if we hear of you going back to your old ways and if you even touch a feather on a bird's body, *WE WILL BE BACK TO DEAL WITH YOU!* Do we have an agreement?' Doolan said. Pebbles had listened intently

'Yes, we have an agreement. I'm sorry, I'll not hurt anyone ever again.' Pebbles was terrified. Plus, had the huge pigeon said there was more of them?

At that, Swifty's machine started to shake and Doolan began to change in size - he was huge, then small, then huge.

'Let's go Doolan!' Twittery shouted, she knew the machine was going to stop working and Doolan would be left down there in his normal size.

Doolan didn't need to be told twice. He flew off. Pebbles looked thoroughly confused. The cat moved over to Mrs Warburton's door and scratched at the glass trying to get in. She had outgrown the cat flap long ago.

CHAPTER 27

The plan is working!

Charlie Sparrow was jumping from side to side, his bright orange bowtie was spinning. Frankie had never seen him so animated.

'I heard them! Loud and clear! The plan is working!' Charlie said, hopping into the air.

'Calm down Uncle,' Frankie said. 'What's happened?' He had no idea what Charlie was saying but it sounded like promising news. In fact, it sounded like fantastic news. He just needed his Uncle to calm down for a moment to let him know what had happened.

'I heard them!' Charlie shouted as he almost twirled in the air.

'Heard who? Tell me what's going on!' Frankie almost screamed. Charlie may have great news, but Frankie was getting frustrated at not hearing what it was.

'Okay, sorry Frankie, I'm just a little excited.' Charlie

said, he had stopped jumping in the air to let his nephew know what was going on. 'I heard Mrs Campbell this morning when I was in her garden having my breakfast. She was talking to her neighbour, Mrs McGinty I think she's called. They were talking about the snowy owls! I even heard them say they can't rip the trees down now. Not with owls living in them!' Charlie almost did a little victory dance.

'That's great news!' Frankie said. 'I just hope they've alerted the powers that be so as the demolition can be called off.'

'I'm certain Mrs Campbell wouldn't allow the trees to be torn down now, not a chance! She'll not just tell her neighbour, she'll let everyone know. I promise you Frankie, there's no way I'm wrong about this.' Charlie flew back into the air and danced back and forth.

Frankie hoped his Uncle was right. He had never seen him so convinced about anything before. After all, the snowy owls had been flying into the human's gardens for hours so surely some of them would have been spotted. It certainly sounded like it from what Charlie was saying. Hopefully the plan had worked but Frankie wasn't going to celebrate just yet. He knew that Crinklebottom was a tricky customer. He had a bad feeling that the rogue property developer wasn't finished just yet.

CHAPTER 28
Inspection of the trees

Crinklebottom had arrived early at the trees with only his hapless sidekick Hobbs in tow. The rest of the workers had refused to come back after being attacked by the magpies. Crinklebottom had planned on instructing Hobbs to smash the trees down with one of the diggers. He had gone through enough. The trees must come down by any means possible. However, just as Hobbs was getting into the digger a crowd of people arrived and that's when things started to go pear shaped.

'You'll need to stop any development right now.' The man in the high vis jacket said. 'We are very lucky to have snowy owls in these here trees!' The man had a pair of binoculars around his neck and a huge smile on his face. He was followed by all the humans who lived near the trees. Mrs Campbell had rounded up everyone just as Charlie Sparrow had thought she would. There were loads of them and they were all eagerly looking into the trees to see if they could spot any snowy owls. They would not be disappointed.

The snowy owls had still been taking it in shifts to fly all over and be spotted. Mildred had watched the crowd of humans with interest and she flew down to a lower branch so as everyone could get a good look at her.

'There's an owl!' Mrs Campbell shouted with glee.

Crinklebottom couldn't believe it. He held his head in his hands. Everything that could have gone wrong with this project had gone wrong and now there were owls appearing as if on demand. He heard rustling in the trees above and suddenly the birds broke into song.

'The birds are laughing at me.' Crinklebottom said to the now bemused looking inspector and onlookers.

'It's okay boss, just a temporary setback.' Hobbs said, patting him on the back.

'Temporary setback?' Crinklebottom said, he was about to give Hobbs a piece of his mind when bird droppings fell from the trees onto his brand-new suit. The crowd laughed at his misfortune. This was not going to plan at all. Crinklebottom closed his eyes for a second and tried to compose himself. Maybe it could be saved he thought, maybe he could come back at night and start a proper fire this time, one that couldn't be extinguished. A proper blaze that would tear down every single tree! A fire so big that no bird or owl would survive! When he opened his eyes again, two policemen had arrived on the scene. This did not look good. Crinklebottom couldn't believe this was happening. These things weren't supposed to happen to him. It was as if the Crinklebottom curse had been reversed and was now hounding him!

'Mr Gerry Crinklebottom?' the policeman said, 'We'd like you to come with us please.'

'What?' Could things get any worse for Crinklebottom? 'I'm not going anywhere.' he said.

'It would be much easier if you would just come down the station and we can sort this mess out.' the policeman said.

The crowd watched on intently. Crinklebottom wasn't listening anymore. He started to make a run for it! Crinklebottom was running in the direction of his van. The two police officers followed closely. There was still a good bit of water on the grass after the birds had extinguished the fire and it had rained earlier - the ground was very slippy! Crinklebottom wasn't going to make it very far. He was going too fast. His left foot slipped first, and he had nothing to brace himself on.

He started flapping his arms and then his right foot went away from under him. He crashed down like a ton of bricks and skidded across the wet and muddy grass, arms and legs flailing in the air. The policemen had stopped chasing him and watched on as he eventually came to a stop in the middle of a muddy puddle. Crinklebottom just lay their covered from head to toe in mud. The crowd couldn't believe their eyes. The two policemen loomed over him.

'I can explain officers-'

'Mr Gerry Crinklebottom, I'm arresting you on suspicion of wilful fire raising, you do not need to say anything but anything you do say may be used in evidence…'

The crowd cheered loudly, and all the birds chirped as the policemen lifted Crinklebottom up from the mud. Yet another one of Crinklebottom's suits had been completely ruined. There was a huge split down the back of his trousers and his bright green underpants were showing this time. The assembled crowd and the many birds in the trees watched on and laughed as Crinklebottom was led to the waiting police car.

There was no way Crinklebottom would be back to tear down any trees now.

The Crinklebottom curse had been well and truly broken.

CHAPTER 29

All's well that ends well

Claude and Cheryl Chaffinch were in the laundry, happy as could be. Their customers could come and go as they pleased. Pebbles had stopped causing them any problems. The cat hardly even came outside anymore. Claude and Cheryl were very busy but that's the way they liked it. Both whistled away happily to themselves as they worked through a massive tower of laundry. It was good to be back to normality.

The wood pigeon school was finally back open for business. Pigeons hustled and bustled in the playground; they were all delighted to be back amongst their friends.

Johnny Fidget and Stevie Starling were working hard in The Bird Stop Café. Fidget hadn't stopped moving all day, he had been running up and down telling every one of the customers that the cafe and the trees had been saved. That his job was safe!

Frankie and Charlie sat with Detectives Doolan and Twittery in the cafe. Not only were the two sparrows busy with lots of cases, now the pigeon police were inundated with work. They had solved the cases given to them by Charlie Sparrow and in the process had proved to everyone that the pigeons could once again be trusted to deal with any crime which was reported to them. There was no chance of Doolan or Twittery being replaced in their jobs now. Peggy Beans and the Owl Parliament had been in touch to thank them for all their hard work.

Even though it was daytime Peggy Beans and other members of the Owl Parliament had joined everyone in the café. The snowy owls had eventually agreed to join the party too. They may have been tired, but they were all having a great time.

Everyone was there. Miles and his pilot friends were sat at a large table devouring an enormous amount of food. Jeff Robin and his family were guests of honour. Even Swifty the Gadget had accepted his invitation.

The birds were having a great time and enjoying the huge feast. They were all having a well-earned celebration.

Pebbles the cat wouldn't be causing any more problems.

The magpies who had been terrorizing humans had decided they would only target humans who were up to no good.

Crinklebottom and his plan for the trees had been foiled.

The trees and the Cafe were being saved from demolition and as for the so called Crinklebottom curse?

It had been crushed once and for all.

THE END

Enjoyed this book?
You can make a big difference.

If you've enjoyed the book, it would be a big help if you could leave a little review or rating (it can be as long or short as you like!)

Thank you very much, it really is appreciated.

Have you read the first Frankie Sparrow adventure?

Frankie Sparrow: Private Investigator

Frankie Sparrow is always getting into trouble. This time he is paying the price ...

It's the school holidays and instead of enjoying himself with friends, Frankie is being forced to get a job.

It's a good thing he's going to work with his uncle, as a Private Investigator!

With a nest-robber on the loose and a missing teacher to track down, Frankie and his Uncle Charlie have no time to waste. However, little does Frankie know that getting a job might just land him in the biggest trouble of his life!

The first book in a laugh-out-loud funny adventure series for 8+ readers from Ewan McGregor, Frankie Sparrow: Private Investigator is action packed with mystery, mischief and mayhem!

Join Frankie on his first adventure today!

Also by this author:

Frankie Sparrow: Private Investigator